THE DREAM TREE

Weekly Reader Books presents

THE DREAM TREE

written by: Stephen Cosgrove
illustrated by: Robin James

This book is a presentation of **Weekly Reader Books.**
Weekly Reader Books offers books for children from
preschool to young adulthood.

For further information write to:
Weekly Reader Books
1250 Fairwood Avenue
Columbus, Ohio 43216

Published by Creative Education, Inc., 123 South Broad Street, Mankato,
Minnesota 56001. Copyright © 1974 by Serendipity Communications, Ltd.
Printed in the United States of America. All rights reserved.

Library of Congress Cataloging in Publication Data

Cosgrove, Stephen.
    The dream tree.

    SUMMARY: Patti Caterpillar resolves to tell her caterpillar friends what
it is like to be a beautiful butterfly when she becomes one herself.
    [1. Caterpillars—Fiction.   2. Butterflies—Fiction]
I. James, Robin,   II. Title.
PZ7.C8187Dr 1979   [E]   78-10866
ISBN 0-87191-665-7

Dedicated to Hazel Stevens, the woman who inspired this book.

Have you ever gazed at a spreading apple tree and wondered how many kinds of life live within its branches? There are probably little black ants, funny little spiders, and, of course, fuzzy caterpillars.

Patti Caterpillar was one of those very same caterpillars, who lived in an apple tree at the edge of a large meadow. She was young, furry, fluffy, and most of all, full of mischief.

All day long Patti would scurry along the branches of the tree, wriggling over and under leaves and twigs. Leaves were her favorite things to wriggle over because they always tickled her tummy.

One day, as she was slipping and sliding on a branch at the far side of the tree, she came upon a large, perfectly white cocoon nestled among the leaves.

Patti studied it, walked around it, but for the life of her could not decide what such a thing would be used for. She was so curious that she began to scurry home to ask her mother.

As she wriggled and giggled her way along the main trunk of the tree, she caught sight of the most beautiful butterfly she had ever seen.

"My!" thought Patti. "How wonderful it would be to soar in the air like that."

She moved closer to the edge of the branch and shouted, "Mr. Butterfly, how did you become such a beautiful butterfly?" The butterfly just floated along on the breeze, and did not answer her.

"Stuck-up old butterfly," muttered Patti.

She then resumed her journey and soon came to her home which was made of leaves. She slipped in the front door and up to her mother. "Mom," she said. "Today, while playing on the far side of the tree, I came upon a white cocoon. What are they used for?"

Her mother sat her down on the toadstool couch and said, "Patti, when caterpillars know that it is the right time, they each go and spin their own white cocoon. Then they slip inside and fall asleep. While they sleep, they dream the dreams of the Dream Tree. When they wake up, they have been transformed into beautiful butterflies."

Patti scrunched up her nose and wiggled her antennae. "That's silly," she said. "Who would ever believe that a furry caterpillar would turn into a beautiful butterfly?"

"But it's true," said her mother. "Someday you and I will be butterflies too."

Patti thought for a moment. "Then how come butterflies don't fly back and tell us what it is like?"

Her mother just smiled and said, "Someday you'll know, Patti. Someday you'll know."

Patti jumped down from the couch and scampered outside. "I think I'll just find a butterfly and ask him what it's like," she said. And with that thought in mind, she headed for the branches nearest the outside of the tree.

She waited and waited, and finally a large butterfly fluttered by.

"Ahem," she said. "Mr. Butterfly, can you tell me exactly what it feels like to be a butterfly?"

The butterfly gazed at Patti and smiled. Then, with a flip of his wings, he caught a passing breeze and floated majestically up and away.

"Mr. Butterfly," she shouted, "why won't you tell me?"

The butterfly from high above said, just in a whisper like the breeze, "Someday you'll know. Someday you'll know."

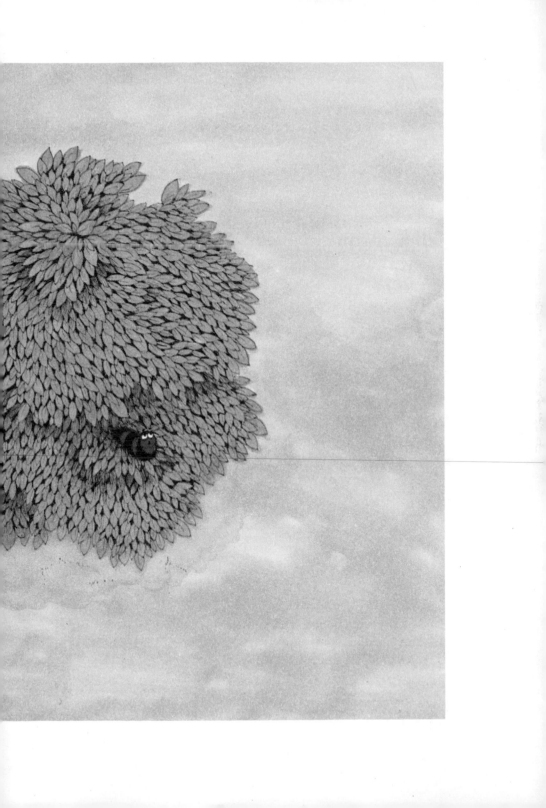

"Oh, darn!" Patti said. "Nobody will tell me!" She turned and wandered over to her favorite twig and curled up. She thought and thought, trying to understand why nobody could tell her what it felt like to be a butterfly.

"I know what I'll do," she said. "When I turn into a butterfly, I'll come back and tell all my caterpillar friends what it's like." Then, contented that she had solved the problem, she closed her eyes and fell asleep in the warm spring sun.

For months thereafter Patti frolicked and played in the tree. But she always kept in mind her promise to herself that when her time came to become a butterfly, she would come back.

Then one day, as Patti was skittering along a branch, she suddenly stopped and her antennae began to quiver.

"It is time," she thought, "for me to go and build my cocoon."

She went to the farthest leaf on the farthest branch and spun herself into her cocoon. When she was done, she fell into a long sleep and dreamed the dreams of the Dream Tree.

After many days of resting, she gently woke up and forced her way out of the cocoon. She felt different all over and she knew that she now was a butterfly.

Patti slowly opened her wings and felt the soft summer breeze begin to lift her quietly into the air and away from the tree.

"Oh, I should go back and tell the others how it feels," she said. "But it feels so wonderful to float in the warm wind." She began to drift up and away, enjoying every motion of her wings.

As she floated upwards, she could see a small caterpillar far below and heard him shout, "What does it feel like to be a butterfly?"

Patti knew what her answer had to be. "Someday you'll know, little caterpillar. Someday you'll know."